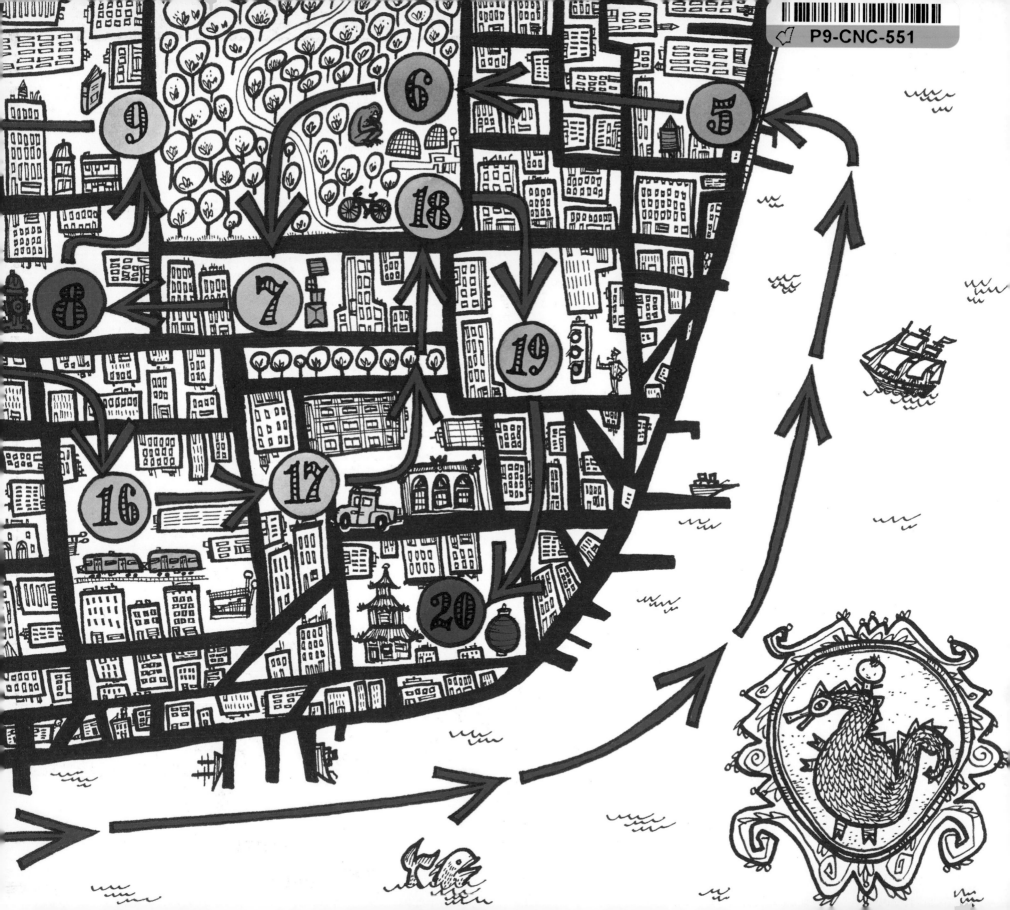

To Olive and Ivy—may the city always be your playground.

First edition 2014

Library of Congress Catalog Card Number 2013943993
ISBN 978-0-7636-6648-4

14 15 16 17 18 19 TTP
5 6 7 8 9 10
Printed in Huizhou, Guangdong, China

This book was typeset in Stempel Schneider.
The illustrations were done in ink using a Mont Blanc 149 with a B nib
that "flips" to a fine line. The nib was adjusted to do so by Richard Binder.
They were then colored using Platinum Mix Free inks.

Candlewick Press
99 Dover Street
Somerville, Massachusetts 02144

visit us at www.candlewick.com

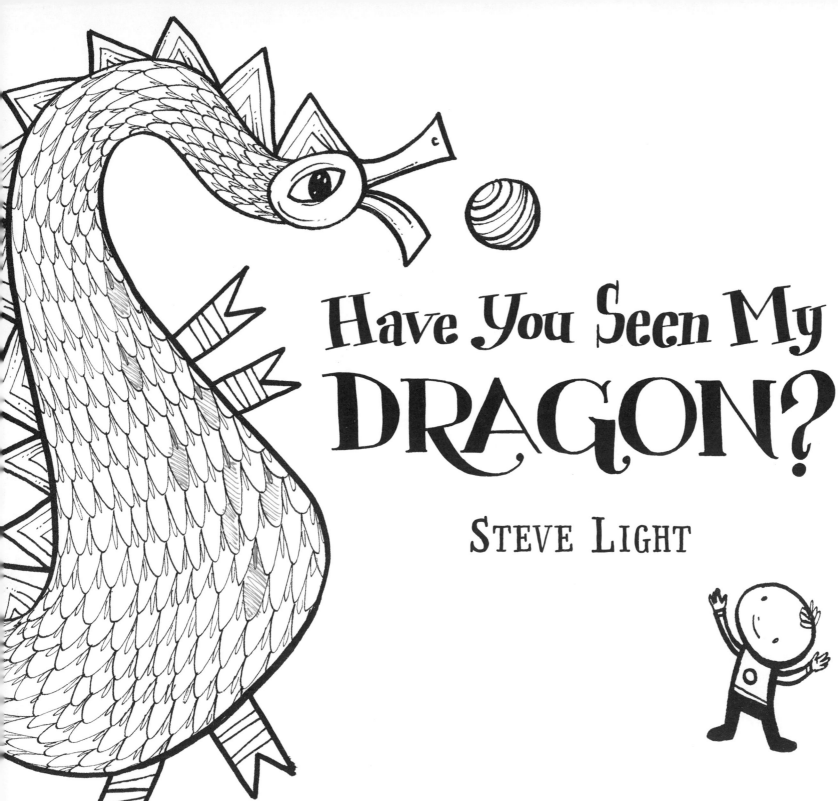

Have You Seen My DRAGON?

STEVE LIGHT

CANDLEWICK PRESS

2016

To Alexandra, Owl Little Dragon. XOXO Dada + Mama

Have you seen my dragon?
No? I will look for him.

2 Hot dogs

Maybe he got hungry
and stopped for a hot dog.

Or perhaps he went downtown on the bus.

3 Buses

4 Sailboats

It's possible he went for a swim.

Or climbed up to get
a drink of water.

5 Water towers

Has my dragon been here
to visit the monkeys?

Could he be
helping the
deliveryman
again?

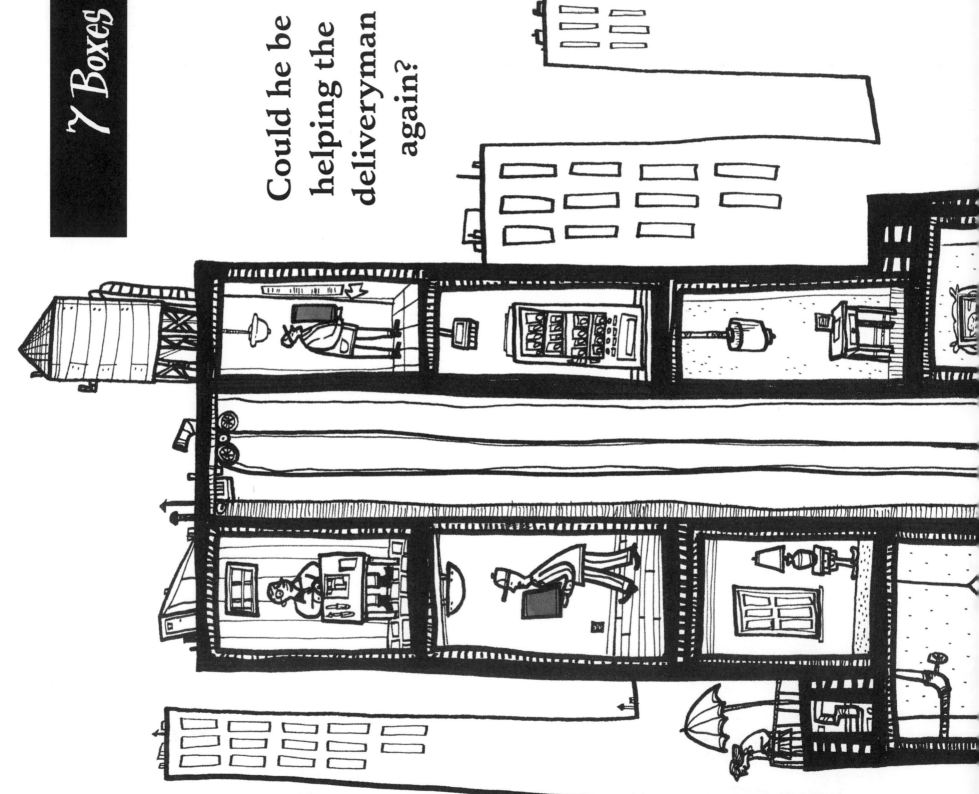

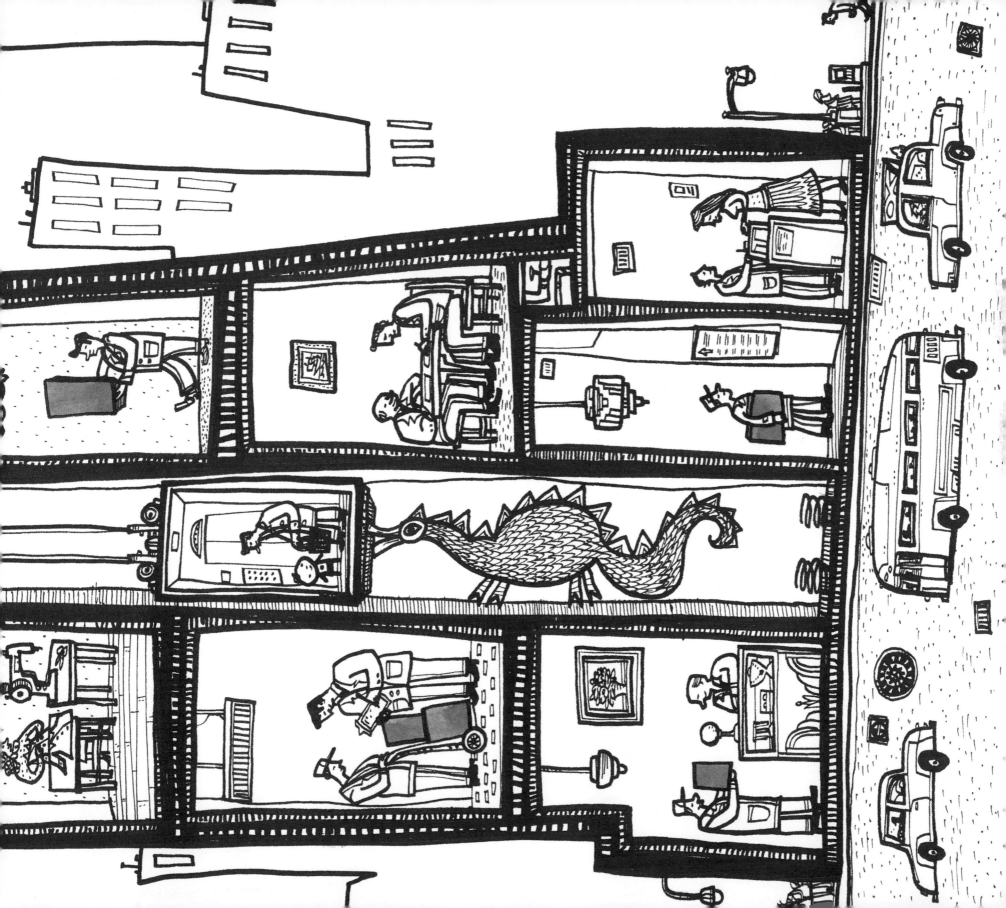

I hope he didn't start a fire with his dragon breath!

I will look at the book stall. My dragon loves to read.

10 Paint cans

Hello!
Has a dragon come through here?

Where could he be?
Down underground . . .

12 Pigeons

or up high
on a rooftop?

I want ice cream!
Maybe my dragon wants some, too.

13 Ice-cream cones

He loves the park . . .

and especially the playground.
Maybe he's there!

Did he go uptown
on the subway . . .

16 Subway cars

or across town in a taxi?

Where is my dragon?

18 Bicycles

There he is!
Right where I left him.